SMARTY PUP

PUP

Pawsome Genius!

First published by Allen & Unwin in 2022

Text copyright © Anh Do, 2022
Illustrations by Anton Emdin, 2022

Allen & Unwin
Dharug Country
83 Alexander Street
Crows Nest NSW 2065
Australia
Phone: (61 2) 8425 0100
Email: info@allenandunwin.com
Web: www.allenandunwin.com

A catalogue record for this book is available from the National Library of Australia

ISBN 978 1 76052 639 9

For teaching resources, explore www.allenandunwin.com/resources/for-teachers

Cover and text design by Jo Hunt
Cover illustration by Anton Emdin
Set in 18 pt Jawbird by Jo Hunt

Printed in June 2022 in China by 1010 Printing Limited

13 5 7 9 10 8 6 4 2

MIX
Paper from
responsible sources
FSC® C016973

ANH DO

SMARTY PUP

Pawsome Genius!

Illustrations by **Anton Emdin**

ALLEN&UNWIN
SYDNEY · MELBOURNE · AUCKLAND · LONDON

ONE

'Hi, my name is Lily!'

Me →

It was show-and-tell day at school. **NOT** my favourite day.

I **never** have anything good to bring in. The other kids **ALWAYS** have something amazing!

You should have seen what Betty brought in last week. Her mum's a vet.

She had a python that needed **six** kids to hold up!

Who wants to play Snakes and Ladders?

The week before that, she brought in the **CUTEST** baby hedgehog!

You know the best way to cuddle a hedgehog? **VERY CAREFULLY!** Hahahaha!

Bruce always has **cool stuff** too. His dad works at a zoo.

This here's a two-headed turtle!

BURP

BURP

And then there's Carla. Her mum owns the town museum so she always has the most **epic** things to show our class.

One time, their butler wheeled in **a real-life mummy!**

Here's the mummy's bummy...

I wished I had something **amazing** to share with everyone. But, last week, all I had to show was...

...A PENCIL.

All the kids **laughed**.

It looked like an ordinary pencil, but it wasn't. My mum had given it to me. It had a pink rubber on the end of it, and Mum used to tell me, **'No one's perfect. We all make mistakes...'**

'...that's what the rubber is for.'

I miss her. I know she would have come up with something really good for me to bring to show and tell today.

'**Next up**,' said our teacher Miss Anne, '**it's Lily's turn.**'

OH NO!

I thought about what Dad had given me for show and tell...**a lousy potato!** Yeah, it kind of looked like an old guy, but it was still just a potato.

'Okay, **Lily**,' said Miss Anne. **'You'll be up
first tomorrow for show and tell.'**

These days, my dad picks me up from school.

My dad is one of those dads who's always trying to make you laugh. **He's actually pretty good at it.**

'I could tell you a joke about this pizza...' said Dad,

'...but it's a little cheesy.'

'I used to not like beards...'

'...but they've grown on me.'

'What do you call an alligator in a vest?'

'AN INVESTIGATOR.'

Sometimes he does **REALLY** funny
things too...
Like when he pulls his 'camel face'.

He's always finding **funny** pictures on the internet, too!

Like this one...

Why the long face?

And he **loves** cat beard photos!

That beard is
PURR-FECT!

He's always looking for something to make me smile. Like yesterday...

'Check this out, **sweetheart!**'

'A potato that looks like an old guy! **HA!** You can take it to show and tell!'

And because I had **NOTHING** better, I tossed that potato in my schoolbag.

Anyway, **here he comes now.**

Hi, Dad.

Hi, Lily.

Dad's always pretty **cheery**, but today there was something **EXTRA** cheery about him.

'I've got something to tell you that you're gonna **love!**' he beamed.

'What is it?!' I asked.

'Well, I know we both really miss being a family of three...' he said.

I had **NO** idea where he was going with this.

'Well,' he said, again. 'We can't bring Mum back...but we **can** be a family of three again...'

We can?

'If we get a **dog!**'

A dog! I couldn't believe it! Mum and I had been dreaming of getting a dog for ages.

'Today's the day, honey!' said Dad. 'I know how much you want one, **SO LET'S DO IT.**'

We're going to get a **DOG!**

TWO

Mum and I used to talk about the type of dog we'd get. She liked fluffy ones, like poodles. Me? I didn't care. I **loved** them all!

My **heart** raced as we drove to the animal shelter and I dreamt about the kind of dog we might find.

Maybe a clever poodle that could do loads of **tricks!**

When we arrived, the first thing I saw was a poodle that looked just like the one I had imagined! **THIS WAS MEANT TO BE!**

RUFF!

But it turned out the poodle wasn't looking for a new home. It **belonged** to the vet who was working at the shelter.

This is my puppy, Cotton Ball!

The dog handler, Sue, led us down a hallway to a room filled with dogs.

I spotted a big black-and-white dog with **amazing** blue eyes. It **wagged** its tail happily when it saw me.

WOW, aren't you **CUTE!**

'Sorry,' said Sue, 'Apollo's already taken.'

Then I noticed a **CUTE** little pug, rolling around and playing with a teddy bear.

'Nope, Buttons isn't available either,' said Sue.

Next, I pointed to a **clever** beagle.

Sue **shook** her head.

NOPE! NOPE! NOPE!

Do you have any that **AREN'T** taken? my dad asked her.

Sue rubbed her chin. She looked around the room, peering past the **husky**, the **pug** and the **beagle...**

'**Ah yes, there's JJ over in the corner,**' she said.

Dad and I stared into the **shadows**.

Slowly, a little pup with a **curl** on top of its head stepped towards us.

RUFF?

It looked up at me with **BIG**, brown eyes.

'This one's probably not the **smartest**,' said Sue. 'But at least he always seems to have a **smile** on his face.'

She leant down and gave the pup a **gentle scratch.**

He **WAS** a **smiley little** thing.

Mum used to say to me, **'You know one of the best things about you, Lily? You've just about always got a smile on your face! And when you smile, I smile.'**

'Let's see what this **little** guy can do,' said Dad.

'SIT!'

He rolled over!

'ROLL OVER!'

He stood up!

'Told ya, not the brightest fella,' said Sue.
'Maybe you can come back next week.
We might have some other options then.'

Sue started leading us away, but I couldn't
help turning back...

The pup was **following us.**

'Um, Dad?' I said, reaching for his arm, when we heard a **HUGE CLANG** behind us!

THUD!

I **ran** back to help the puppy.

'There you go, **little** buddy,' I *whispered* as I lifted the bucket off his head.

He looked up at me with the

BIGGEST SMILE...

Dad **crouched** down beside us.

'I **WANT** him,' I said to Dad.

'Are you sure?' he asked.

I rubbed the pup's ears and he **smiled** again.

I always try to look for the **good** in everything. This dog might not have been the **cleverest**, but there was something about his face that made me feel really **happy** inside.

Can we **PLEASE** take him home with us?

Dad **winked** at me. 'We'll take him!' he said.

'**Oh, great, okay,**' said Sue.

'Hello JJ!' I said. 'Your name is **perfect**, because my dad's name is Jerry and my mum's name was Jennifer. You're going to be part of our family now.' I looked into his **BIG gorgeous** eyes.

After we left the animal shelter, we took JJ shopping! Firstly, we had to get him a kennel.

There were **LOADS** of fancy ones.

BARKINGHAM
PALACE

And then there was **this one...**

'What do you think, JJ?' I asked.

JJ **wagged** his tail.

Then he walked right into the fake door on the side...

THUD!

'OOPS, that's not the door, JJ! You go through this way,' I said, showing him around to the opening.

I think he liked it. He was

GRINNING FROM EAR TO EAR!

We bought him some other doggie things, like snacks and a collar...**and then I spotted some outfits!**

'Can we, Dad? **PLEEEEASE?'**

Dad **nodded** and tossed me a **cowboy costume.**

GIDDY UP PUP

Cowboy JJ! →

Mermaid JJ!

'He looks **CUTE** in every outfit!' said Dad.

JJ then **wandered** over to a green striped t-shirt, so we thought we'd try that out.

As soon as it was on, he gave us a **HUGE smile**. So we bought that one!

When we got home, we all had **dinner** together.

JJ was a **VERY** messy eater. Twice he ended up with the **bowl** stuck on his head!

How **adora–bowl!**

Pretty soon it was time to take JJ out the back to **sleep** in his new kennel.

THUD!

I looked at Dad and **shrugged**. 'We might need to paint over that fake door.'

Once more, I helped JJ around to the
actual kennel opening. He **wandered** in
and curled up in a **cosy** ball. He looked really
sleepy.

'Goodnight, JJ!' we called, before heading
back inside.

Thank you,
Dad.

In the middle of the night I woke to a **LOUD CLAP** of **THUNDER**. It sounded really stormy outside.

I **hoped** JJ was okay out there.

In the morning, there was no sign of last night's storm. The sun was **shining bright**. It was the **perfect** day for a girl and her dog!!

Where could he be?

I was **searching** the yard when I realised the back door to our garage was open...

Who had opened it? I was pretty sure Dad was still **asleep** upstairs...

From the doorway, I noticed boxes **spilled** on the floor and books **scattered** everywhere.

And then I saw him...sitting on a chair in the corner.

'Ah, good morning, Lily!' said JJ.

I **rubbed** my eyes. Was I **dreaming?!**

But he was **STILL** there.

'Lily? Are you **okay?**'
he asked.

'**You look a little pale**,' he said.

'Did you just...**talk?**' I asked.

'**Why, yes, I did**,' JJ replied.

'**WHAT IS GOING ON?!**'

'**Well**,' said JJ, 'allow me to explain. Last night during the storm, a **blob** of purple **goop** from outer space fell on me.'

'I'd just stepped out of my kennel for a quick stretch, when

SPLAT!'

'**It's all over the news!**' he said. Then he picked up the remote and **switched on the TV.**

'A **meteor** shower from deep **space** hit Earth overnight,' said the reporter, 'carrying with it a purple alien **GOOP** that has caused **unusual** things to happen around the world.'

'There are lots of reports of people developing **strange** skills.'

The reporter turned the mic to a man on his doorstep.

Yesterday I definitely could not speak Chinese. But this morning I woke up and **NOW I CAN!**

'Wǒ zhēn bang!' he said. 'That means I'm **AMAZING!** in Chinese!'

Next, the reporter approached a **little** old lady.

'I've never been very **STRONG**,' she said, quietly. 'But I woke up this morning and...'

...now
**I CAN
DO
THIS!**

Back to you in the studio!' said the
panicking reporter.

'See?' said JJ. 'I'm not the only one!
All my life I've wanted to be **clever**.
I guess that alien substance last night
has helped my **wish come true**!'

'Ask me anything! **Go on!**'

'What's **55 x 55?**'

'3025. **Too easy.**'

'Who's my dad's **favourite** superhero?'

'Thor.'

'You really **DO** know everything!'
I exclaimed.

JJ chuckled. '**Ha, not really. I guessed
that last one. Everyone loves Thor.**'

Suddenly, I **heard** Dad **calling** from the kitchen. 'Lily! Breakfast! Come on, I gotta get you to school on time!'

'**School! Great!**' said JJ, **LEAPING** off the chair. '**I've always wanted to go to school!**'

'I hope there are quizzes!'

'Huh?' I said. 'Oh, no, you can't come to school with me. You're staying **right here** until I figure out what on earth is going on...'

'Why can't I come with you?'

'Well...because I've got **show and tell** today and all I have is this old potato...and I was hoping... **WAIT** ...hang on...'

I've got show and tell today and I've got a **TALKING DOG?!?**

'Okay,' I said, 'you're coming with me. But first, we **need** to talk to Dad.'

Dad was at the stove **boiling** eggs when JJ and I walked in.

'Dad, don't **freak** out...but there's **something** I need to tell you,' I said.

'And what **eggs—actly** is it?' asked Dad.

I wasn't sure how to say it, so I just blurted it out. **'JJ can talk now!'**

'That's great!' he replied. 'Let me guess; he can say **ROOF** and **BARK**?'

'No, talk as in **talk**,' I repeated.

In a few different languages, **ACTUALLY.**

'Ooh, is that boiled egg?' JJ asked.
'I've always wanted to try **boiled egg!**
Can I please have some?'

My dad looked **COMPLETELY** puzzled as he handed a peeled egg to our talking dog.

'Here you go...'

JJ **tossed** the whole thing into his mouth.

'This is **DELISH!**' he cried, **smacking** his lips.

And at that point, my dad **fainted**.

THUD!

'Come on, Dad, **get it together**,' I said,
fanning him with a tea towel. 'You need to
get up and take us to school! I'm taking JJ
for **show and tell!**'

THREE

Dad drove us to school in a bit of a **daze**, as JJ and I **chatted** away in the back. He kept looking at us in the rear-view mirror and **shaking** his head.

'A **talking** dog? I'm going **BARKING** mad!' he muttered to himself.

'Are you **SURE** this is a good idea, Lily?' Dad asked.

'It's a **GREAT** idea,' said JJ, full of confidence.

'It'll be fine, Dad,' I agreed.

I helped JJ into my backpack, leaving an opening for his head to stick out.

'Okay, now remember, I need you to pretend you're a normal dog until it's time for **show and tell!**'

'**Ruff!**' said JJ with a grin.

Bye, Dad!

Bye!

I felt like **skipping** across the playground, I was so excited to have JJ with me!

We were halfway to the classroom when a stray cat ran past us. JJ suddenly **LEAPT** into my arms!

EEEEK!

My old potato **TUMBLED** to the ground.

'Cuddle me, Lily!' JJ cried.

He was **TERRIFIED!**

'What's wrong?' I asked. 'Don't tell me you're scared of cats?!'

I **DON'T** like cats at all! I'm very very **SCARED** of cats! They give me the hiccups! **HIC!**

'It's okay, JJ,' I said. I had to promise him the cat was **long gone** before he agreed to **hop** back in my bag.

I picked up the old potato and **walked** to class.

'Sorry, old man spud,' I said as I **tossed** the potato in the bin.

I found my desk and sat down, carefully popping my bag by my feet.

'It's Lily's turn for **show and tell**,' said
Miss Anne, and I smiled back at her. I picked
JJ up out of my bag.

Everyone **OOHED** and **AHHED**, like he was
a **cute** and completely normal dog.
JJ was **cute**, but he sure wasn't **normal!**

'Hi everyone, I'd like you to meet my
new dog.'

'Hello class, my name's JJ!' he said.
The class nearly fell to the floor in **surprise!**

'Did he just **TALK?'** asked Miss Anne, **gobsmacked**. 'Did your dog...just **TALK?!'**

'**I sure did!**' said JJ, happily. He **hopped** up onto Miss Anne's desk. '**So, this is what a classroom looks like,**' he added, looking around the room. '**Amazing**.'

Everyone **rushed** over to hear more. They had a **MILLION** questions!

Kid: 'How long have you been able to talk?'
JJ: **'Since this morning!'**

Kid: 'What's it like being a dog?'
JJ: **'I used to spend a lot of time digging holes, but now I prefer reading books!'**

Kid: 'Why do you sniff other dogs?'
JJ: 'Um, probably because we can't shake hands!'

Kid: 'Do you like eating dog food?'
JJ: 'It's not bad, actually, but my favourite food now is **EGGS! Eggs are yummy!**'

The class went **ballistic!** They **loved** JJ! Just like I knew they would!

It was turning into a real

JJ PARTY!!

'Excuse me, Miss?' interrupted Carla.
She looked a little cranky. 'I **also** have
something **amazing** for **show and tell**.'

I could tell Miss Anne **didn't want to
stop** chatting with JJ, but Carla was right
– it was her turn.

JJ and I returned to my desk.

Emma leaned over and *whispered* to us.

'Best **show and tell EVER.**'

Carla **shocked** everyone when she
presented... **Gregg the Egg!**

'Gregg is a **GIANT** T-Rex egg and the
official mascot of our town.

'My mummy, the museum owner, said I
could bring it in today,' said Carla.

'It's **millions** of years old,' she explained.
'And **EXTREMELY** fragile.'

We couldn't believe **Gregg the T-Rex Egg** was right here in our classroom! This egg was **more famous** than **Humpty Dumpty!** All of us were **impressed**. Even the cleaner, who was out in the hallway, popped his head in.

'Is that **THE** Gregg Egg?! **WOW!**'

'Elwood **used** to be famous for interesting **pies**...' said Carla. 'People used to come to our town to try **all** the different types'

'There was the **Ice Cream Pie**, the **Candy Cane Pie**, the **Hotdog Pie**.'

'But since **THIS** was discovered in our town,' she said, cradling the **T-Rex egg**, 'everyone comes to Elwood to see our famous **egg**!

'Now we have...

'**1.** The Giant Revolving **Egg** Restaurant'

Come in for a **SPIN!**

I hope it doesn't spin too fast, or it'll be **SCRAMBLED** egg!

'2. The **T-Rex Egg** Museum'

Our egg display is hard to **BEAT!**

'3. And the Annual **T-Rex Egg** Parade!'

And now, an **EGGS**-quisite song from our Tyranno-**CHORUS!**

'**Look at the size of that!**' JJ said to me, as Carla carefully rested the **egg** on the stand on the bookshelf. '**Imagine that** egg with a bit of salt and pepper...'

Mmm.

Some kids turned around to **glance** at JJ.

At lunchtime, **everyone** wanted to play with us.

Lily! JJ! Over here! Want to play?

JJ was having **the time of his life!** And I was **too.**

He joined in with **skipping...**

This is so much better than **CHASING STICKS!**

And he was soon teaching **US** some **tricks!**

They were **REALLY** hard.

Maybe we should **SKIP** those tricks...

We played **TAG**...

JJ was **SO FAST!** I think one of his

ancestors must have been a greyhound!

No one was **SAFE!**

GOTCHA!

We showed JJ some other **FUN** schoolyard stuff.

Like **Smell the Cheese...**

ARGH!

...and playing **marbles**.

JJ was **REALLY** good at it. His little
ears **twitched** as he worked out how to
throw his shooter marble.

'JJ,' I said, 'you're a walking **CANINE** calculator!'

'Well, do you know what you get when you cross a **dog** and a **calculator**? A best friend you can **COUNT ON!**'

'All this running around has made me hungry,' said JJ.

'I've got some **doggie biscuits** in my backpack,' I told him.

'**Can I go grab them?**' asked JJ.

'Of course,' I said, and JJ **DASHED** back to the classroom.

In moments, he was **TROTTING** back, **chewing** and **trailing** crumbs across the yard.

When the bell rang, we walked back to class together. We could see there was some sort of **commotion**...things were being **flung** all over the place!

What **was** going on?

Carla was **shouting** something about the **T—Rex egg**.

'Where is it?! **WHO** has taken it?!' she was **screeching**. 'My mummy will **NOT** be happy about this!'

WHO HAS STOLEN GREGG THE EGG?!

FOUR

'It's okay, Carla,' said Miss Anne. 'We'll find it. The principal's on his way.'

Carla was searching the room, eyeing everyone **suspiciously**. The egg stand was still there on the shelf, but it was **EMPTY**.

'YOU! Belinda!' she called. 'What's that in your bag?'

Belinda's backpack had a **BIG** egg-shaped **bulge** in it.

'This?'

'It's my **ball!**'

'And what's **THAT?'** Carla **shrieked**, pointing to Jeremy. His jacket was **bulging** in the front.

'Nothing!'

'Just an **afternoon snack!**'

What's going on here?' said Principal Taylor, as he entered the room. 'Is it true our town's **mascot** is missing?!'

JJ and I looked at each other. Where could it have gone? **WHO** could have taken it?

Suddenly, Ronnie stepped towards Principal Taylor. 'I think **I** know who took it,' he said.

And would you believe it, he turned around and pointed...

...at **JJ!**

WHAT?!

'I certainly did not!' scoffed JJ.

'JJ said his favourite food is **EGG...**' said Ronnie. 'He was practically **DROOLING** over the **Gregg Egg** earlier today!'

'You're right,' added Sarah. 'He said it just needed **SALT** and **PEPPER!**'

'He's probably going to **eat** it for dinner!' added Ronnie.

Principal Taylor pulled out his phone. 'Security! I **need** you immediately!'

'Somebody call the dog catcher!' he said.

'NO!' I cried. 'JJ didn't take the egg!'

'It was a joke!' said JJ. '**I wouldn't EAT** that egg. That thing's a million years old! I'm a talking **dog**, not a **caveman!**'

'Where did you put it?' Carla **demanded**.

JJ just looked at me and **shook** his head.

'Oh,' said Carla, 'suddenly you're not so good at talking, **huh?'**

'This is a very **serious** matter!' said Principal Taylor. 'Everyone is to drop everything and search for **Gregg**. It's the pride of our town and it must be found.'

'Whoever finds it, I give you my word, will be **rewarded** with **ANYTHING** they want!'

With that, everyone **rushed off** to start searching.

Just as I was trying to work out what to do, Security showed up and Principal Taylor told them to **take JJ away!**

'Lock this dog up in storage until the dog catcher gets here!'

'No!' I shouted. **'STOP!'** But they grabbed JJ and carried him away.

Get your hands off me!
I'M INNOCENT!

'We'll sort this out, JJ!' I called.
'I promise!'

Miss Anne put her hand on my shoulder.
'I'm sorry, Lily, but the dog catcher will be
here soon to take JJ away. I'll let your dad
know.'

I wandered outside as **everyone** around
me ran **wild** trying to find the **egg...**

I couldn't **believe** everyone thought JJ had done something with it.

I was starting to feel like I might **cry**, when suddenly I heard **barking**.

It was coming from the storage room in the corner!

JJ?

'I'm here!' I **whispered,** up against the locked door.

'Lily!' said JJ. '**Wanna help me get out of here?**'

'Of course, but **HOW?!** You need a **code** to open this door!'

'**I have it! I saw the code the guard punched in,**' said JJ. '**I watched the reflection in his sunglasses!**'

'5243...'

It worked! The door unlocked!

CLICK!

JJ ran out. '**If we can solve this mystery together,**' he said, '**everything will be okay again. Do you trust me?**'

'Of course I trust you,' I said. 'But we **DON'T** have long. The dog catcher will be here at any moment.'

'**We need clues...**' said JJ. '**Fast!**'

'**To the classroom!**'

Everyone was still **RUNNING** around the school, **searching** for the **egg**. But our classroom was empty. **PERFECT!**

'**What's this?**' said JJ, picking up a jacket near the empty **egg** stand. '**That wasn't there before.**'

'It belongs to Tom,' I said.

We found Tom in the playground.

'Okay, I admit, I did go back to the classroom during lunchtime,' said Tom, 'but only to drop off my jacket. **It was hot!**'

'**So you didn't touch the egg?**' said JJ.

Tom **screwed** up his face then **BLURTED OUT**, 'Okay, okay, I did, but I just wanted to hold it for a second. Then I put it right back, **I swear!**'

'Did you put it back on the wooden stand, or just on the shelf?' said JJ.

'I...was **RUSHING**...I think I just put it back on the shelf...'

'So it was lying on an angle?'

Tom nodded.

Back in the classroom, JJ stood by the shelf and **scratched** his chin.

'So the egg was at an angle, perhaps a 30-degree tilt...so it might have been **a little wobbly.**'

He dropped to the floor and started looking under the desks.

'I don't see it down here anywhere, but...'

'...I see **wheel marks!**'

Wheel marks? What could they be from?
No one had a **skateboard** or **bike** at
school...

'**That's it!**' said JJ.

'The cleaner's **been in here!**'

'He must have come in during lunch to
empty the bin,' he explained. '**You threw
an old potato in here earlier, and it's
GONE.**'

JJ was right!

But did he think the cleaner had **stolen Gregg?!**

'He must have wheeled the trolley along here, next to the shelf,' said JJ, '**and stopped it RIGHT on this spot to go and grab the bin...**'

'...where these marks turn.'

JJ's ears were **twitching**. I could tell his mind was trying to work it all out.

'And the **shaking** of the trolley could have been just enough to set the egg slowly rolling down the shelf...' he said.

'To land...'

'...IN THE CLEANER'S TROLLEY!'

'So he **didn't** steal it?!' I said.

'**No**,' said JJ. '**I bet he doesn't even know he has it!**'

We **RACED** through the hallway, searching for the cleaner and his trolley.

'They're here, JJ! **The dog catchers!**'

'We need to find that cleaner and clear your name, **NOW!'** I cried as we ran.

When we **finally** found him, the cleaner was making his way down the hill with his trolley. He was heading for the **GARBAGE CRUSHER!**

We ran to him as **FAST** as we could. **'Hey! Don't go any further!'** shouted JJ, and the cleaner turned around.

It looked like JJ – my **talking** dog - gave him a **FRIGHT!** The cleaner stopped in his tracks, **threw his hands in the air...**

AND LET GO OF THE TROLLEY!

The trolley **ROLLED** down the hill, picking up pace! **We raced after it!**

STOP THAT TROLLEY!

Suddenly, there was a loud **SCREECH!**
The dog-catcher van pulled up next to us,
and a guy with a **HUGE** net jumped out!

STOP THAT DOG!

'No!' I cried. 'We have to stop that **TROLLEY!'**

It was getting **closer** and **closer** to the garbage crusher!

Just as it was about to **CRASH** into the crusher, the trolley hit a rock and **JOLTED** to the right...

PHEW!

But then it **SMASHED!** right into a bench!

SMASH!

OH, NO!

EVERYTHING shot up into the sky... including the **egg!**

Gregg the Egg SOARED through the air... then **PLUMMETED** *FAST!*

It came down and hit...

...the playground trampoline!

BOUNCE!

We kept **RUNNING** towards it as it **BOUNCED** up and onto the second trampoline...

BOUNCE!

...and then up and heading for the third.

I **BOLTED** around to catch it...**but missed!**

OOPS.

'I've got this,' said JJ, who **SKIDDED** to a stop. He stepped back and watched the **egg** soaring into the sky. His ears started **twitching**.

'I've worked it **out!**'

'According to my calculations,' he said, 'the **egg** should **hit** that swing, **roll down** the slide, **bounce off** the rope climber, **flick off** the spinner...'

Sure enough, the **egg** started **BOUNCING** and travelling just as JJ had said! We **DASHED** across the playground to try and save it!

The dog catcher was right behind us! **He almost had JJ!** I was torn between the flying **egg** and JJ!

The dog catcher **DIVED** for JJ, so I turned and **LEAPT** in front of him.

OOF!

The dog catcher and I **TUMBLED** to the ground. I **rolled** and **crawled** as quickly as I could out of the net.

The **struggle** gave JJ just enough time to **SNATCH** up the net, **SPIN AROUND, RUN UP** the slide to **LEAP OFF THE TOP...**

...and **CATCH** the **T-Rex egg** right in the centre of the net!

'Got it!'

The **egg** was safe! JJ had saved it!

WOW!

Just then, a **cat** walked past and JJ **freaked** out, launching the **egg** into the air again!

This time I **BOLTED**...

...and caught it
in my arms!

PHEW!

I looked up and realised that everyone had gathered around us.

'**EGG**-cellent catch, Lily!' shouted Carla.

All the kids as well as Miss Anne **AND** Principal Taylor started **clapping.**

HOORAY!

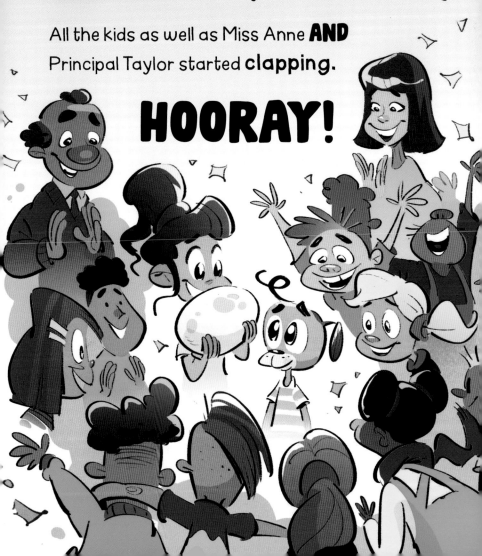

FIVE

Show and tell had almost turned into a complete disaster! But we'd saved **Gregg the T-Rex Egg** and proven that JJ had nothing to do with its disappearance!

The dog catchers were still lurking, but
Principal Taylor told them they could leave.
'These two just saved **Gregg the Egg!**'

He then turned to me and said I'd earned
whatever I liked.

Would you like a new
schoolbag? Free lunch
for a week?

But I knew exactly what I wanted.

'I'd like JJ to join our class,' I said.

'Sorry?' said Principal Taylor. **'That's not possible.** The kids and teachers would never want–'

'**Have you asked them?**' said JJ.

'I can **guarantee** you, a dog in the classroom is the last thing they'd want,' said Principal Taylor.

'LET'S GO TO A VOTE,' he boomed, turning to the crowd. 'All those in favour of allowing Lily to bring her **strange-looking** dog to school each day, please raise your hands.'

There was silence.

I looked at JJ and **shrugged**.

'I'd **love** it,' said a small voice. An arm was in the air.

It was Timmy.

'Me too,' said Miss Anne, raising her arm as well. 'JJ's kinda **awesome**.'

Suddenly the school broke out in unison. **'LET THE DOG STAY! WE LOVE THE DOG!'** they chanted.

'JJ!' **'JJ!'** **'JJ!'**

I turned to JJ, who had the **BIGGEST smile** on his face. It was so **BIG**, it made **me** smile too.

SIX

That evening, the three of us sat at the
kitchen table together, eating dinner.

'You've cooked **eggs**, Dad!'

'Yep,' said Dad. 'Why don't **eggs** joke around?' he asked.

'**I don't know,**' said JJ. '**Why?**'

'Because they'd **CRACK** each other up!' said Dad.

HA! HA! HA!

'I'm so **glad** you joined our family,' I told JJ.

'**Me too,**' he replied. '**I love** it here.'

'But we might need some more **books!**'

JJ had **already** made his way through every book in our house, including the old phone books!

Dad and I **glanced** over at the photo of Mum on our wall.

'You know what, JJ?' I said. 'I reckon Mum would have **loved** you.'

At that moment, the neighbour's **cat** **JUMPED UP** to our kitchen windowsill. JJ shrieked!

HEEEEK!

HAHAHA!

'I **love** you, JJ.'
'I **love** you too, Lily.'

THE END

BOOK 2 COMING SOON!